See Ice, Think Twice

Danielle Alise Dunlap

Illustrated by Karen Kohler Kaiser

This book belongs to:

_____

Stay Safe!

This book is dedicated in loving memory to my Aunt Kathy and cousin Kadin.
Miss you both...

Last night it snowed and the ground is now a blanket of white.

Sam and Max are building a snowman outside with their dog Cooper.

It is cold outside today, but thankfully, their mom bundled the boys up with warm coats, scarves, and hats.

"We need a hat for our snowman," Max says.

"He can use mine," offers Sam. Sam lets Max put the hat on their snowman's head. "Now he is done!" Max declares proudly.

Sam and Max's little sister Molly joins them outside and has brought her sled.
"Let's go sledding!" exclaims Molly eagerly.

"Look at our snowman Molly," states Max, "Isn't he great?"

"Yes, but let's go sledding!" Molly shouts growing impatient.

"Ok,ok," says Sam, "We will go."

So Sam, Max, and Molly head for
the snowy hills behind their house with
Cooper following behind them.

"Ok Molly, you can go first." states Max. "I will give you a push,"

"Weeeee!" squeals Molly as she slides down the hill.

Sam, Max, and Molly take turns pushing each other down the hill with Cooper chasing them down each time.

They are all laughing and having fun until Molly falls off her sled and it glides onto the frozen lake. The lake has become icy from the recent cold weather and is also covered with a layer of snow.

"Oh no, my sled!" shouts Molly.

"Don't worry Molly," says Max. "I'll get your sled." Max starts walking toward the frozen lake.

"No Max, STOP!" shouts Sam. Cooper starts barking loudly to alert Max.

"We need Molly's sled." Max says as he continues toward the lake.

"STOP, Max!" repeats Sam.

Max finally stops and looks at Sam.
"You NEVER go on the ice," states
Sam. "I learned about this in class.
The only safe ice is on a skating rink ."

"Max, you could fall in the cold water and get hurt. So remember, if you ever fall in icy water be calm, kick your feet, pull yourself up out of the water and through the ice opening where you fell in, and roll off the ice.

- Calm
- Kick
- Pull
- Roll

Ice is dangerous!

"But my sled," utters Molly sadly.
"Don't worry Molly, we will tell Mom and-
Dad about your sled," says Max.

"Remember, when you see a frozen lake, think twice about going on the ice," says Sam as they all walk to the house to tell their mom and dad about Molly's sled.

This book was inspired by the drowning deaths of Kathy and Kadin Baxmeyer and his friend Austin. The three of them fell through thin ice on Kadins 7th birthday, February 19th, 2010.

About the Author & Illustrator

"A mother -daughter duo"

Danielle Dunlap earned a bachelor's degree in elementary education from McKendree University in Lebanon, Illinois. As a full time mom of three, she understands the importance of teaching safety to her children. In an effort to raise awareness of ice safety steps , she has authored an easy-to-read story. Her mother, Karen Kohler Kaiser, illustrated the images.

The author and the illustrator's goal is to stress the need for children to stay off ice and be safe around frozen water.

Self rescue steps if you fall through ice into water...

* ## Stay Calm

* ## Kick feet like a swimmer -horizontal

* ## Pull yourself up on the ice while kicking

* ## Roll off ice after exit, never stand up!

color me!

See ice, Think Twice

* Stay Calm

*Kick

*Pull

*Roll

Made in the USA
Monee, IL
06 December 2019